First American Edition 2016
Kane Miller, A Division of EDC Publishing

Text © 2016 Pippa Goodhart
Illustrations © 2016 Sam Usher

Published by arrangement with Egmont UK Ltd
The Yellow Building, 1 Nicholas Road, London W11 4AN

For information contact:
Kane Miller, A Division of EDC Publishing
PO Box 470663
Tulsa, OK 74147-0663
www.kanemiller.com
www.edcpub.com
www.usbornebooksandmore.com

Library of Congress Control Number: 2015954259

Printed in China
3 4 5 6 7 8 9 10

ISBN: 978-1-61067-512-3

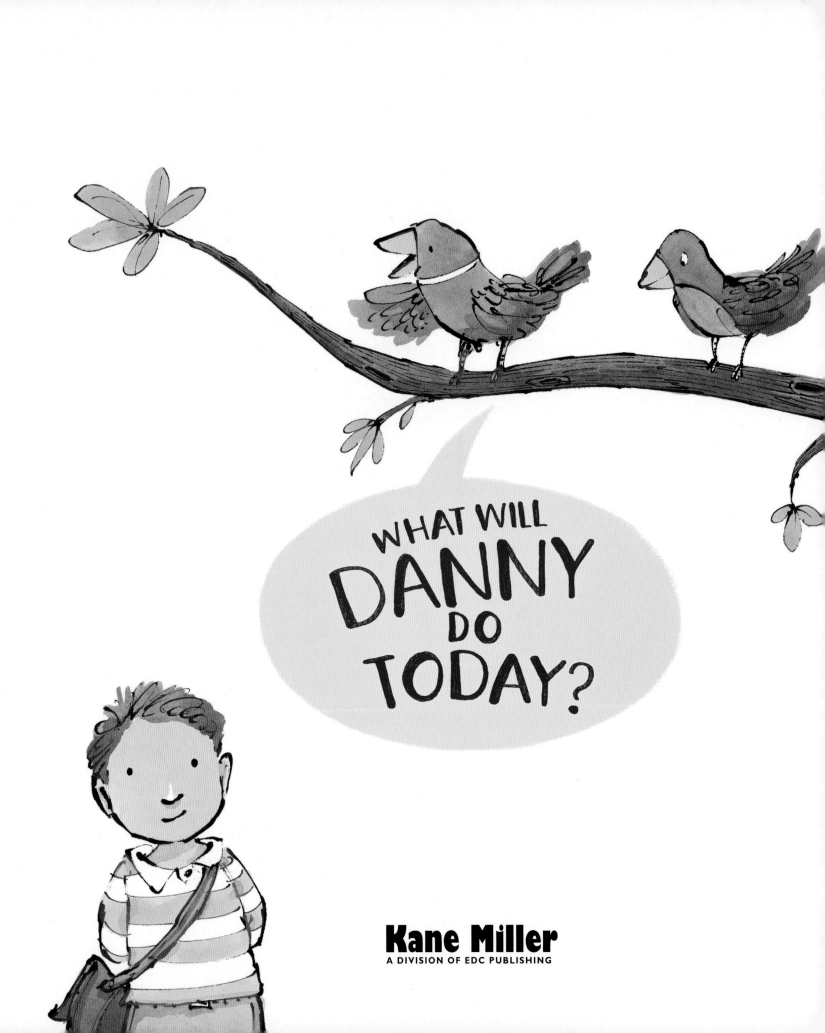

WHAT WILL DANNY DO TODAY?

Kane Miller
A DIVISION OF EDC PUBLISHING

What will Danny wear today?

Will he choose spotty, stripy
or plain clothes?

Will he pick a crunchy,
chewy or wobbly breakfast?

100 CAKES

What do you think he'll drink?

After Danny has waved good-bye to his dad,
will he pedal or zip, walk, ride or skip to school?

SCHOOL

What will Danny learn?

Rocket building? Painting?

Or playing the piano?

Who will teach Danny today?
And who do you think his
favorite teacher is?

LOST MUG

When it's time for PE
will Danny run, jump
or hit balls?

Will he slide, swing or seesaw at recess?

In the afternoon, everyone is cutting or sticking or painting.

What will
Danny make?

Danny's dad is picking him up after school. He's wearing a green jacket – can you see him?

Will Danny skate, row or watch a movie for his special treat after school?

After his busy day,
which book will
Danny take to bed?

Look! He's chosen the
one that you've just read!